The
Not-So-Jolly
Roger

THE TIME WARP TRIO

The
Not-So-Jolly
Roger

by Jon Scieszka

illustrated by Lane Smith

VIKING

Special thanks to the Brooklyn Public Library

Title hand lettered by Michele Laporte.

VIKING
Published by the Penguin Group
Viking Penguin, a division of Penguin Books USA Inc.,
375 Hudson Street, New York, New York 10014, U.S.A.
Penguin Books Ltd, 27 Wrights Lane, London W8 5TZ, England
Penguin Books Australia Ltd, Ringwood, Victoria, Australia
Penguin Books Canada Ltd, 2801 John Street,
Markham, Ontario, Canada L3R 1B4
Penguin Books (N.Z.) Ltd, 182–190 Wairau Road,
Auckland 10, New Zealand

Penguin Books Ltd, Registered Offices:
Harmondsworth, Middlesex, England

First published in 1991 by Viking Penguin, a division
of Penguin Books USA Inc.

3   5   7   9   10   8   6   4   2

Library of Congress Catalog Card Number: 90-51008
I S B N   0 - 6 7 0 - 8 3 7 5 4 - 7
Printed in U.S.A.   Set in 13 point Sabon

For Jake

ONE

I thought you said you read *The Book*," said Sam.

I looked over at Sam and Fred swaying in the tops of the two coconut trees next to mine. We were thirty feet above the ground. I grabbed my tree tighter. "I did," I said weakly. I closed my eyes so I couldn't see just how far up we were.

"Well, what happened this time, Mr. Magic?" asked Fred. "We didn't even open *The Book!* We were just goofing around in your room. Now we're making like monkeys in the tops of some trees on a deserted island."

"Maybe it was something you said," said Sam.

Waves crashed on the beach. I smelled the salt air. I opened one eye to look at Sam and Fred. Sam's glasses hung from one ear. Fred's Mets cap was twisted backward. They did kind of look

1

like monkeys hugging coconuts. If I hadn't been so scared, I would have laughed.

"I said I read *The Book*. I didn't say I understood it."

"Oh, great," said Sam, trying to hang on to his coconut and fix his glasses at the same time. "So you're telling us you don't know where we are?"

I looked out at the long stretch of blue ocean. The hot sun hung high in the blue sky. I tried to guess what time it might be.

"Where we are? I don't even know *when* we are."

"*Aaaaaaaaaaaaaah!!!*" screamed Sam.

A red and blue parrot flew by and screeched back.

"We're lost," moaned Sam. "Shipwrecked. Castaways. Robinson Crusoes in time and space. We have no idea where or when we are. *Aaaaaaaaaaaaaah!!!*"

"Get a grip," said Fred. "I wished for buried treasure. *The Book* sent us here." Fred started to climb down his tree. "It doesn't take Einstein to figure it out. Somewhere around here there's buried treasure."

2

"We are going to die," said Sam. "Don't say I didn't warn you. Because where there's buried treasure, there's pirates. We are dead meat. Shark food."

"Well, look at the bright side," said Fred. "If you're dead, you won't have to go to school Monday."

Sam gave his glasses a push. "Ha. Ha. Ha. You're so funny, I forgot to laugh."

Fred started to slide down the tree trunk. "What's the big deal? We find the treasure, dig it up, Joe says the hocus-pocus stuff, and we go back home millionaires."

"Well . . ." I said.

"What's this 'well?' " said Sam. "I don't like the sound of this 'well.' "

"Well, *The Book* says there are a lot of ways to travel in time," I said. "But the only way to get back to our time is to find the person who has *The Book* in this time."

"But what about the All-Purpose Time Warper Spell?" said Fred.

I shook my head. "It only works going backward. We have to find *The Book* to get home."

3

Sam knocked his head on the nearest coconut. "Oh, fine. That's just fine. I mean, that should be easy. Thanks to lame-brain treasure hunter here, there aren't that many people to ask for *The Book*. Let's see . . . we could ask this coconut. We could ask that sea gull. We could ask the ocean. We could ask the . . . oh, no."

"What's an ono?" I asked.

Sam pointed out to the ocean.

We could just see the front of a sailing ship appearing from around the edge of the island.

"Hey, it looks like a ship," said Fred.

"Three guesses what kind of ship, Einstein," said Sam. "And the first two don't count."

We clutched our trees and watched the front of the ship turn into what looked like a huge wooden ocean liner. Except this ocean liner had cannons. And it was flying a flag from its mast— a black flag with a white skull.

"Oh, no," said Fred. He went back up the tree. Fast.

T W O

While the pirates drop anchor and load their rowboat, maybe I should back up and explain how we three guys happened to find ourselves up in the coconut trees and in big trouble two hundred and seventy-five years before our time. It was just a week after the last time we travelled through time. And that was more than a thousand years before this time, which is a later time if you're just reading this for the first time in your own time, which . . . oh, forget it. Let me start one more time.

Last week (my time), I got a birthday present from my uncle Joe. Uncle Joe is a magician. He gave me a book. It had strange silver writing on the front that said *The Book*. When Fred opened *The Book,* it transported my two best friends (Fred and Sam) and me to King Arthur's time. We met a bunch of knights, a dragon, a giant, and stuff like that. But you can read about that some other time.

To get back to this time, the week after we got back to our time, Fred and Sam came over to my house to check out *The Book* again.

"I've been thinking about this time travel stuff," said Fred. "And I think we should go somewhere worth our while." Fred sat on my bed, still wearing his baseball uniform, tossing his baseball up and catching it. "Kids in those magic books I've read are always so dumb. They always wish for exciting adventures or some garbage like that. And they never take anything useful with them—like a machine gun or a jet. I say we wish for a pile of money and come back millionaires."

Sam looked up from his comic book. "No way. It will never work. If you had ever made it to the end of any of those magic books, you would know that magic is very tricky. Like Joe's uncle said, 'be careful what you wish for. You might get it.' We could wish for a pile of money, end up in a bank, and get shot by Jesse James."

I sat at my desk, trying to perfect my disappearing quarter trick. "Sam's right. It's not like faking people out with coin tricks. Let's just be a little more careful this time and figure out exactly what we're going to wish for."

I looked at the midnight-blue book on my desk.

"Magic can backfire on you even when you're trying to do good," said Sam. "And it will definitely mess you up if you are greedy."

"So, Mr. Know-It-All, what do you want to wish for?" asked Fred, pulling his baseball cap down over his eyes.

"I think we should go visit some famous historical figure and see what they were really like."

Fred threw his ball up to the ceiling and caught it. "Go visit some famous historical figure? Get out of here! You should be in one of those other lame magic books with all the other stiffs. Who wants to go visit famous dead guys?"

Sam pushed his glasses up. "I do."

"Get a life," said Fred. "So we go visit George Washington. We come back. What do we got? Nothing. But, we go visit buried treasure. We come back. What do we got? Millions!"

"Oh, that's brilliant, Sherlock. This is the same kind of bright idea that almost got us executed last time. Did you ever stop to think who buries treasure? Pirates, that's who. And do you know what pirates usually have? Pistols and cutlasses, that's what. And do you know what they do with those pistols and cutlasses? Shoot and stab people who are trying to steal their treasure, that's what."

"Come on," said Fred. "I took care of the Black Knight, didn't I? What's a few pirates? Joe, you got any pictures of buried treasure in that book?"

I stuck the quarter in my pocket and picked up *The Book*. "No."

"So there," said Sam.

Fred cocked his arm to throw his baseball at Sam.

"But there is this spell called the All Purpose Time Warper:

Hickory dickory dock.
Mouse, turn back the clock.
The clock won't strike.
To go where we like—"

"Buried treasure," yelled Fred.

"No, you jerk," yelled Sam.

Fred threw his baseball. Sam ducked. Wisps of pale green mist began to swirl in my bedroom.

"But wait," I said, "the spell only works—"

Fred's baseball slowed and then froze in mid-air, only inches away from my desk lamp.

The Book seemed to melt right out of my hand.

The green mist swirled faster and higher; covering book, ball, bedroom, and all.

THREE

Oh, no is right," said Sam.

We looked around the island for somewhere to hide. The choices were pretty slim: our three trees, or one big black rock.

We climbed higher into our trees, and did our best to look like coconuts. We couldn't see anything, but we could hear the splash of oars and bits of some truly awful singing.

What do you do with a drunken pirate?
What do you do with a drunken pirate?
What do you do with a drunken pirate
Ear-ly in the morning?

The small rowboat landed as I peeked through the leaves. Two guys unloaded a chest. One was tall. The other was short. Both wore ragged pants and striped shirts. They were the ugliest and nas-

11

tiest-looking guys I've ever seen . . . until I saw
the third guy behind them. He was twice as big
and twice as nasty-looking.

He was the one with the awful singing voice,
and boy, did he have a face to match. Black hair
stuck out everywhere. His black eyebrows and
moustache bristled out front. Long black strands

fell down his back. And a monstrous black beard, with four pigtails, braided and tied with ribbons on the ends, fell down his chest. To top it all off—the whole mess was smoking!

But the worst part about this guy was not his crazy hair or black outfit. The worst part was that he was equipped, just as Sam had predicted, with four pistols and one wicked-looking cutlass.

"Bad luck," whispered Sam. "I'll bet anything that's Blackbeard . . . and not the Walt Disney version."

"Who's Blackbeard?" Fred whispered from his tree.

"His real name was Edward Teach," said Sam. "Some people say he was the craziest and meanest pirate of all time."

"Oh," said Fred.

The two ragged guys staggered up the beach lugging the chest between them. The giant black pirate counted off paces behind them.

"Eighteen, nineteen, twenty, twenty-one. *Halt!*"

They stopped right under our trees.

"Dig here, lads. We bury our treasure, and we three be the only ones what know about it, eh?

Who says I don't treat me prisoners well? Have another tot o' rum."

The big guy pulled a bottle out of one of the deep pockets in his long coat. He took a swig, and passed it around.

The two prisoners drank, then started digging.

The pirate leaned against my tree. The top of his three-cornered hat was right below me. Something in his hair *was* fizzing and smoking, and it smelled terrible. I wiggled my nose as quietly as I could, and tried not to think about sneezing.

The pirate jabbed the sand with his cutlass. Then he started in with that singing again.

> *Come all you bold rascals what follow the sea,*
> *To me way, hay, blow the man down,*
> *Haul in yer sails and now listen to me,*
> *And give me some time to ya de dee dee . . .*

"Just us three, eh, laddies? Not a soul around."

Sam and Fred looked at me and bugged their eyes out.

The hot sun beat down. Flies buzzed around. The prisoners drank and dug. The bearded pirate kept singing—horribly. My foot, wedged behind a coconut, went to sleep. My arms felt like they were going next. Finally, after what seemed like hours, the two guys finished digging. The pirate slid his cutlass back in his belt.

"Yar, mates. That would be perfect. Now lower her in there slowly, slowly . . ."

While the two prisoners were lowering the chest, the pirate pulled out two pistols and shot them both.

The bodies and chest fell to the bottom of the hole with an ugly thud. The crazy pirate laughed and started croaking another song as he kicked sand in the grave.

Sixteen men on a dead man's chest,
Yo, ho, ho and a bottle of rum.
Drink and the Devil will do the rest.
Yo, ho, ho and a bottle of rum.

A drop of sweat rolled off my nose and fell down toward the singing pirate. It landed right on his hat. I closed my eyes and held my breath.

He stood up, looked all around, and said, "Just us three, lads. Guard our secret well. Har, har, har." And then he turned to go.

That's when the fly decided to land on Fred's nose.

Fred wrinkled his nose, blinked, and shook his head.

The fly flew.

Fred's Mets cap slid right off his head, spinning down, down, down, until it landed with an awful *plop* right at the toe of the pirate's big, black boot.

He froze. He looked at the hat. Then he looked slowly up, up, up the trunk of my tree. Our eyes met and my heart went as numb as my foot. The black pirate growled, *"Arrrrrrrgh,"* and grinned a crazy smile. I swear I saw his eyes flashing red.

Then he pulled out two pistols, aimed, and fired.

FOUR

*C*lick, went one pistol.

Click, went the other.

"Damnation and hellfire. Forgot to reload. But you won't be going nowhere, will you now, lad?"

My brain thought about diving out of the tree. My body refused.

The pirate tossed the two empty pistols aside and reached for two more.

While he was reaching, Fred slid down the trunk of his tree and jumped to the sand. "Don't shoot! That's my hat."

The pirate whirled around and aimed the pistols at Fred. "Yarrr, this island be haunted, sure. They're dropping from the trees. Quick, lad, how many more of your kind up there?"

"Two," said Fred.

"Three against one? Why, those are the best

odds I've had in a long time." He tucked away one pistol and drew his cutlass. "Call out the rest of your spying monkeys. Let's fight to the death and the Devil take the hindmost."

Suddenly Sam spoke up. "But we can't fight you."

The pirate squinted up into the trees. "What's that? What do you mean you can't fight? Why in Hades not?"

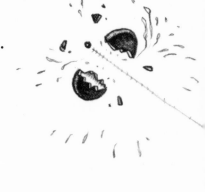

"We can't fight you because . . . uhh . . . because we'd lose our Magicians' License," said Sam.

"What?"

"Yeah, that's it," said Fred. "We're magicians—magicians from another time, and it's against Magic Rules for us to mess with anyone because we are so powerful."

"Magicians, eh?" The pirate itched his chin with the barrel of his pistol. "I'm a bit of a magician myself. See that coconut? I'll make it disappear." He fired his pistol. The coconut Fred had been sitting behind exploded in a shower of milk and shredded coconut.

The giant pirate laughed a scary, crazy laugh. "Now get your magic selves down here where I can see you."

Sam and I started down as fast as we could.

"Thanks, Sam," I said.

"And you best have some stronger magic than that," he yelled, "or you'll be disappearing, too. Har, har, har."

"Thanks a whole lot, Sam."

At ground level, the guy looked even bigger, meaner, and uglier than from above. He did have some smoking rope hanging in his hair. He did have pigtails in his beard. And he did have crazy-looking red eyes. The pirate slung his pistols and looked the three of us over with those eyes. He lifted Fred's hat from the sand on the tip of his cutlass and jabbed it at him.

"So you three pips are magicians from another time, are ye?"

He stared at Fred in his baseball uniform. Thin wisps of smoke curled up around his three-cornered hat. "And does everyone dress this funny in your time?"

Fred pulled on his hat and muttered, "Look who's talking."

21

"What was that, lad?"

"Oh, I said . . . enough talking."

"Right you are," said the pirate, towering over us. "So let's see some magic. Otherwise I might be thinking you were just spying on me and looking to steal a bit of me buried treasure." He smiled his nasty smile again. "And if I thought that, I'd have to kill you right now."

Fred gulped. "Uh. . . . Eenie, meenie, mynie, mo. Catch a pirate by the toe. If he hollers, let him go. Eenie, meenie, mynie, mo!" Fred pointed to Sam. "Sam will now show you his powerful magic!"

The pirate wasn't smiling anymore.

Sam stepped forward on wobbly legs.

"Uh . . . hi, there, uh . . . Mr. Blackbeard," said Sam.

The pirate's dark face went suddenly white. "How do you know my name?"

"I read it," Sam said.

"Where's your crystal ball?"

"Oh, I don't need one. I even know your real name."

"Do you now?" Blackbeard looked around, then bent forward. "And what might it be?"

"Edward Teach."

Blackbeard staggered back a step and looked over his shoulder. "The Devil you say. You lads *are* magic."

My uncle Joe always says to work the crowd when you've got them believing. I saw my chance to impress Blackbeard even more with our "magic."

"And what's that in your boot?" I said.

The big pirate looked down and jumped. "What? What?"

I reached around his boot and held up a quarter.

Blackbeard snatched it out of my hand and gave it a close look. "What strange doubloon is this? That wasn't in my boot before."

Blackbeard stared at the quarter in his hand.

"You mean you lads can use your magic to pull pieces of eight right out of the air?"

"Oh, sure," said Fred. "That's nothing for powerful magicians like us. We could do that all day long."

"Could you now?" Blackbeard looked us over carefully.

We took a step back.

"I could use a few mates with your talents."

The three of us began to back away slowly.

Blackbeard slid his cutlass into his belt and put the quarter in his pocket. "Why don't you join me aboard my new ship?"

"Oh, we'd love to, but I have a . . . a . . . a big history report due Monday," said Sam.

"I call her the *Queen Anne's Revenge*." Blackbeard pulled another loaded pistol from his endless collection and pointed it between my eyes. "Do you think that's a nice name?"

I looked down the barrel of the biggest pistol I've ever seen.

"That's a very nice name," I said.

"Its previous owner ran into a bit of trouble . . . if you know what I mean."

Sam looked down the length of the cutlass. "I know what you mean."

"Would you like to join me on board then?"

Fred looked at Sam and me.

"We'd love to."

We marched down to the rowboat—the pirate ship anchored in the bay before us; Blackbeard, his loaded pistols, and his awful voice behind us.

Come all you bold pirates what follows the sea,
To me way, hay, blow the man down,
Just get me some magic and treasure for me,
And give me some time to blow the man down . . .

"Pirates didn't really make guys walk the plank, did they?" asked Fred.

"Nah, that's just in the movies," I answered, hoping it was true.

FIVE

*A*aaaaaaaaaah!!!!"

"Heads up, lads,"
yelled Blackbeard.

We grabbed the rope
ladder and flattened
ourselves against the
side of the *Queen
Anne's Revenge.*

A blindfolded
man fell past us. He
landed with a splash and
then disappeared beneath the waves.

Fred turned as white as the guy's
blindfold.

"Blast it all," growled Blackbeard. "If
that sea-rat crew of mine walked all the
prisoners off the plank, I'm going to

26

have to cut off some heads. Up you go, lads."

We climbed up the side of the ship so fast we didn't even have time to be afraid. But there was plenty of time for that once we climbed over the rail and stood on deck. Because there, eyeing us like hungry sharks, were at least a hundred black, white, and every different shade of brown, pirates.

I didn't see any wooden legs, earrings, eye patches, or hooks. But I saw as many daggers, knives, swords, cutlasses, and pistols as you'd ever want to see.

The owners of this dangerous collection of hardware and the three of us stood frozen, staring at each other wide-eyed and open-mouthed. Then Blackbeard jumped over the rail behind us.

"*Israel! Israel Hands!*" yelled Blackbeard. "You scumbucket, low-life, fish-bait son of a wharf rat first mate—what in the name of the Devil's hind end is going on here?"

A long-haired pirate stepped forward. "Just a bit of fun to pass the time, Captain."

"*Bit of fun?!*" yelled Blackbeard. "You bilge water-brained idiots! Those prisoners were worth their weight in gold ransom! You just walked a fortune off the plank for a bit of *fun?!*"

Blackbeard stomped back and forth. He slashed the air with his cutlass, and swore a five-minute string of curses (too nasty to be written down in any book) at his first mate and crew.

"And now I might ask you barnacles for brains—where might we find our next treasure?"

The first mate and the wild band of cutthroats looked at their feet.

Fred, Sam, and I did our best to shrink into the background.

Blackbeard drove the point of his cutlass into the deck with a loud *thunk*.

Blackbeard looked out over his crew.

Then he smiled that devilish smile.

"I'll tell you where we get treasure, mates."

The crew looked up.

"I'll tell you where we get more treasure than a king's ransom, more treasure than El Dorado, more treasure than all the gold on these Seven Seas."

"All right," said Fred. "Now we're getting somewhere."

Blackbeard pulled his cutlass out of the deck and pointed it at us. "There."

We gasped.

The crew murmured.

"Who'd pay anything for those three?"

"They look sickly to me."

"That's one's a prisoner. Look, he's still got a number on his shirt."

Blackbeard smiled. "Gentlemen, we are about to become retired pirates. No more long, boring sea voyages. No more fighting for measly treasures. No more dodging the King's warships. And no more worries about ending your days swinging from the end of a hangman's noose."

I started to get what Blackbeard was leading up to.

I started to get a serious stomachache.

"These three lads may look a mite strange," continued Blackbeard. "That's because they are. They are time-traveling magicians. And they can pull doubloons out of thin air."

The crew roared.

"Show the magic," said Blackbeard, and he stuck one of his huge boots forward.

"All right, Joe," whispered Sam. "Stall them with your quarter trick. We'll think of something."

"I don't have it," I said.

"What do you mean you don't have it?" said Fred.

"My quarter, I don't have it. Blackbeard took it, back at the beach."

We all dug into our pockets. Not a penny.

I tried to think of another trick that might work. Pick a card? These guys didn't look much like card players. The disappearing quarter? No, it had already disappeared.

"Heave ho," yelled a member of the audience. "Out with the magic, already."

"Ladies and gentleman," I began, stalling for time. "Well, I guess just gentleman, really. Maybe I should say fellows. But that really doesn't sound much like the beginning of a magic show. I always like to start my magic shows with 'Ladies and gentlemen.' So does my uncle Joe, now that I think of it—"

"Stow the gab," yelled a coal-black guy with a knife.

"*Razzzerfrazzerrowwowarrrgh,*" added his friend with a pistol in his belt.

I broke out in a sweat.

The already-ugly crowd got uglier.

"Fake!"

"Forget the pieces of eight," said a nasty-looking one-armed fellow. "Let's see some real magic. Let's see if they can fly off the plank! All in favor, say 'Aye.'"

The yell that went up from the crew was the loudest (and scariest) "Aye" I've ever heard.

"You're not feeding me to the sharks," yelled Fred, and he made a break for it. He jumped up the rigging and started to climb. A pirate with a white scar running from where his ear should have been to his chin, grabbed Fred's foot and threw him down to the deck with a laugh.

"Now, just a minute," said Sam. "You can't just toss innocent people overboard."

"Brethren-of-the-Coast Rules, mate," said Blackbeard. "We all votes to decide what goes. The captain only gives the orders in battle. Show your magic, or walk the plank."

"But—" said Sam.

And in seconds, the three of us were standing on a plank, hands tied, twenty feet above the deep blue water.

"Bring the blindfolds," said Blackbeard.

"Some movie," said Fred.

SIX

We can't die," said Fred. "This is supposed to be magic. Joe, say one of those spells or something quick."

I closed my eyes and tried to remember The Industrial-Strength Time Freezer Spell.

> *Hey, diddle diddle,*
> *The cat and the fiddle.*
> *The cow now stops the moon.*

I opened my eyes. For just a second, everything fuzzed out of focus like a cheap TV set. I thought I saw a bit of green mist swirling on the ocean. No such luck.

Then the lookout sang out from above, "Sail off the port bow! Sail off the port bow!"

Blackbeard looked through a spyglass. "She's flying the British colors. One of the King's warships out fishing for pirates." Blackbeard lowered the spyglass and laughed. "Looks like we're in for a fight. Cast off the anchor, Mr. Hands. Hoist sail and run right at 'em. Load cannon on both sides, and we'll meet our friends with a broadside on whichever side they turn."

The first mate went into action, yelling stuff that sounded like English, but didn't make much sense. "Drop the deadman! Hoist top, main, and royal! Load and tackle batteries port and starboard!"

The men swarmed all over the deck and rigging, pulling ropes, lifting sails, loading cannons. Blackbeard leaned his elbows on the rail and watched the approaching ship.

There was a jolly pirate,
He sailed upon the sea.
He packed his cannons full, boys,
And met the King's na-vy.

"And Mr. Hands—stow our magicians in the aft hold. We'll tend to them later."

The first mate pushed Sam, Fred, and me toward the back of the boat.

Some of the men were rolling big brass cannons up to hatches in the side of the ship and tying them down with ropes and pulleys. Others were soaking blankets and draping them over the sides and all around a small cabin on deck.

"Oh, this is a fine time to be washing blankets," said Sam. "We're about to be attacked by the King's Navy, and these guys are doing their laundry."

"That's the powder magazine they're wetting down, lad. If that gunpowder catches fire and blows, none of us ever needs do our laundry again."

Mr. Hands laughed, opened a hatch in the deck, and shoved us in. The three of us tumbled down some narrow steps and landed in a heap.

"Ow," said Sam.

"We are definitely in trouble now," I said.

"Yeah, thanks to Fred, Time-Traveling Treasure Hunter, here," said Sam, "we're trapped in Blackbeard's hold with a British warship about to blast us out of time and space."

"Blackbeard won't get caught. He's a famous historical person," said Fred.

"Great," said Sam. "If we don't get blasted out of the water or hanged for being pirates, we'll get to walk the plank."

"So?" said Fred.

"So?" yelled Sam. "You got us into this whole buried treasure mess and all you can say is 'So?'"

"Guys, guys," I said. "Our only hope is to find *The Book*. We have to think. Where would it be?"

We sat quietly in the smelly, dark hold and tried to think.

Cannons rolled and men shouted overhead. The ship rocked.

"I've got it," said Sam. "The captain's quarters. That's where they always keep the ship's log and maps and things."

"That's got to be it," I said.

"Let's go," said Fred.

"I think you're forgetting a few things," I said.

"Like: our hands are tied, the hold is locked, the ship is covered with pirates, and we don't even know where the captain's quarters are."

We could feel the ship roll and pick up speed.

"Well, it's a good thing some of us came prepared." Sam held up two pieces of rope in one hand and his Swiss army knife in the other.

"All right!" said Fred. "We're out of here."

Fred jumped up the stairs and pushed his back against the hatch. "Come on and push, you guys. I think we can spring it."

Cannons boomed above us and rocked the ship sideways.

"If we get out of this alive, Fred," said Sam, "I'm going to kill you."

We were halfway up the steps when we heard the return cannonfire from the British ship. Three seconds later, everything exploded.

Light and smoke and noise poured in. Up above, men were screaming, yelling, and groaning. I sat up and threw a splintered board off my leg. "Are you guys okay?"

"Ow," said Sam.

Fred, stretched out face down at the foot of the steps, didn't say anything.

SEVEN

Sam stared at Fred's motionless form.

Guns and cannons fired. The ship rolled.

"Fred, I didn't mean it," said Sam. "Fred, are you okay? Speak to us. I promise I'll never say anything mean to you ever again."

Sam lifted a board off Fred's back.

"Ow," said Fred.

Sam punched him. "You moron. We thought you were dead."

Fred sat up and rubbed the back of his head. "Nah. It takes more than a cannonball to knock off a time-traveling magician."

Up where the hatch used to be, now there was a jagged hole. We could see smoke, sails, and sky.

"Let's get out of here and go find *The Book*,"
I said.

Sam looked up and gave his glasses a push up
his nose. "On second thought, maybe we should
just wait it out down here."

Fred and I pushed him up the stairs.

The hold was noisy, but up on deck was like
a scene from hell. The smoke and smell of gunpowder was everywhere. The full crew of some
two hundred pirates swarmed all over the ship.
Some were throwing buckets of water to put out
small fires on the deck and in the sails. Others
rolled the cannons back to load them. Still others
were up in the rigging, cutting free damaged lines
and sails. Guys with muskets lined the rail on
one side and kept up a steady stream of fire at
the British ship blasting through the sea along-
side. Bullets and metal pieces zinged by, ripping
holes in the sails, shredding rope, and splintering
wood.

Sam's idea to wait out the battle in the hold
suddenly seemed like a great one.

We crouched behind a stack of barrels. Sam
pointed to a small door at the very back of the
ship. "The captain's quarters."

The only problem was, standing there in front of the door, coat, hair, and beard flying, firing pistols with both hands, and cursing his head off, stood the captain himself—Blackbeard.

We tried to hide. But then, as if he felt our eyes watching him, he turned and saw us. He gave us his scary, crazy grin and started making his way toward us through flying bullets, cannonballs, smoke, and men. We were trapped like rats.

And that's when it happened.

The pirate at the cannon closest to us stood up and lit the cannon fuse. A bullet hit him and knocked him back. He fell on the guy holding the cannon rope, and they both went down.

The loose cannon rolled back, spun around, and came to a stop pointing directly at the powder magazine.

The fuse burned lower.

Blackbeard shouted, "No!"

The four pirates at the next cannon dove overboard.

Fred jumped down to the cannon. "Come on, guys! We've got to turn it!"

Sam and I ran over and pulled the cannon rope. Fred pushed. And with one heave, we twisted the cannon just as it fired.

The blast knocked us off our feet and sent the cannon crashing backward. We watched the cannonball fly up and then fall gently down. We heard a crash, wood splintering, and then saw the mainmast of the British warship slowly lean and fall like some giant white-leafed tree. The huge ship heeled over and dragged to a stop with half its sails in the water.

The pirate crew cheered and yelled as we raced out to sea. Blackbeard and the guys who had been ready to toss us overboard ten minutes earlier, helped us to our feet.

"That was one bold move with a loaded hundred-pounder, lads," said Blackbeard. "You're welcome to join me crew, and ask any favor of me you wish."

Fred's eyes lit up. I knew exactly what he was thinking.

Before he could say anything, I asked, "Do you have a small book, about this big, dark blue with gold stars and moons along the back edge, and twisty silver designs on the front and back?"

Blackbeard scratched his still-smoking beard.

"A book? . . . a book." Blackbeard yelled out to the crew gathered around, "Does any of you swabs got a book?"

"We had a book once," said the first mate. "But the preacher that brought it took it off the plank with him."

"Could you take us home to New York then?" asked Sam, before Fred could open his mouth.

"Sorry, lad," said Blackbeard. "If we sailed into New York, me and this whole bloody bunch would be swinging from a noose in a minute."

Fred looked at Sam and me. We couldn't think of anything else. We were about to become full-time members of Blackbeard's pirate crew.

"Well, then," said Fred. "Maybe you could give us a bit of . . . buried treasure?"

"Yaaarrrrrrr!!!!" Blackbeard roared and clapped Fred on the back. "Spoken like a true pirate, lad. It's buried treasure you want? Buried treasure you get."

EIGHT

Blow the man down will ya, blow the man down
Way hey blow the man down.
Just get me that treasure from out the cold ground
And give me some time to blow the man down.

Fred wore Blackbeard's three-cornered hat. Blackbeard wore Fred's Mets hat. And they sang together in awful disharmony. The red sun sank slowly toward the ocean. Sam and I rowed the small boat toward shore.

"I knew Blackbeard was an awful pirate," said Sam. "But I never read anywhere that he was such a terrible singer."

I thought about the two pirate prisoners who had been sitting in our seats earlier in the day. "Probably because nobody ever lived to tell about it."

Blackbeard took another swig from his bottle
of rum and started singing again.

Sixteen men on a dead man's chest.
Yo, ho, ho, and a bottle of rum.
Drink and the Devil will do the rest.
Yo, ho, ho, and a bottle of rum.

"You know," said Sam. "I read once that a
dead man's chest is another name for a coffin.
That's how sixteen men can fit on one."

I rowed a few more strokes and watched the sun going down. "That's great."

I turned and looked at the huge pirate laughing and singing with Fred. Something about his eyes and the red light from the sunset shining off his pistols made me nervous.

Sam leaned over as he pulled his oar and said what I was thinking.

"I don't trust this guy. All the legends and books say he was one of the nastiest pirates who ever lived. Why would he be taking us to a deserted island to give us some of his treasure?"

I remembered the sound of the two guys falling on top of the chest.

"Because he likes us?" I said.

Sam rolled his eyes.

We hit the beach and followed Blackbeard and Fred. We walked toward three familiar coconut trees.

"Fifteen, sixteen, seventeen, *halt!*"

We stopped about ten paces away from the old treasure hole.

I was relieved that we didn't have to dig up any dead guys.

"Dig here, mates, and the treasure is yours."

Blackbeard and Fred sang. Sam and I dug.
The scene seemed unpleasantly familiar.

"Watch your back," said Sam. "I think we're
digging our grave."

The sun sank until it hung balanced on the
horizon.

Then, to our surprise, about three feet down,
we hit wood.

"Buried treasure!" yelled Fred.

Blackbeard smiled. "Lift her out slowly."

We cleared the sand from around a small chest and lifted it up.

Blackbeard slid a hidden button and popped up the lid. His smile suddenly turned to a frown.

"*Arrrrrgh*." The red light of the setting sun shone in his eyes as he looked up at us. "Some thieving rats have been gnawing at me treasure."

We looked in the chest. It was empty except for a small package wrapped in black cloth.

"But who could have stolen the treasure on this deserted island?" asked Fred.

Blackbeard looked at us. "Who, indeed? Maybe some spying monkeys, hiding in them coconut trees."

Sam lifted the package out of the chest.

Blackbeard pulled out two pistols and leveled them at us. "Maybe these three spying monkeys."

Fred held up his hands. "Oh, no. You don't think we took your treasure."

Blackbeard turned toward Fred. "If there's one thing I hate, it's a treasure thief."

The black cloth fell
from the edge of the
package in Sam's hand
and showed a corner of blue.

"Man, you must be crazy," said Fred. "We never—"

"Get over there," thundered Blackbeard. "Stand by your grave with your thieving mates and say good-bye."

I ripped the cloth off the package. It was a book—a thin blue book with moons, stars, and strange silver writing.

It was *The Book.*

In my hands it fell open by itself to a picture of three familiar guys.

The sun set behind the ocean.

I heard a shot.

And the wonderful green time-traveling mist swirled up over us all.

NINE

*C*rash.

Fred's baseball smashed my lamp into a hundred pieces.

The last few bits of mist disappeared slowly like the tail end of a dream.

Sam sat on my bed looking stunned.

We looked at each other, then around my room.

"Where's Fred?"

"Oh, no," I said. "You don't think he got—"

Sam nodded.

"What are we going to tell his mom?" I said.

"Joseph Arthur? What in the world are you boys doing in there?"

My mom.

"If that was your desk lamp I heard breaking, you are in big trouble, young man."

"What are we going to tell my mom?"

"Joseph? Frederick? Sam? Are you boys in there? Answer me."

I put my hand on the thin blue book on my desk.

"Maybe we can go back to just before the pistol shot," I whispered.

Sam nodded. "We have to go back and get him."

"Boys?" The doorknob began to turn.

I reached for *The Book*. A baseball hat and a head appeared from under my bed.

"Ow," said Fred.

TEN

Historical Afterword

Blackbeard, somewhat shaken by his encounter with the Trio, swore off drinking and pirating, got rid of his forty-gun ship, the *Queen Anne's Revenge,* and his three-hundred-man pirate crew. In June, 1718, he received his Royal Pardon from the Governor of North Carolina and settled in the town of Bath, North Carolina, as Edward Teach, Retired Pirate.

He should have stayed that way.

But he didn't. I guess he got bored. He started pirating again. On November 22, 1718, Blackbeard faced Lieutenant Maynard of His Majesty's Royal Navy in the Battle of Ocracoke Inlet. Blackbeard lost the battle, his life, and his head (which Lt. Maynard hung from the bowsprit of his ship). Legend has it that when Blackbeard's headless body was tossed overboard, it defiantly swam around Lt. Maynard's sloop several times and then sank.

For roughhousing indoors with guests, **Joe** was sentenced to one weekend of manual labor, cleaning and organizing his room (closet and desk drawers included) under his mother's supervision.

Fred was lectured about playing outdoor games at the appropriate time and in the appropriate place. He was given the choice of helping **Joe** clean or paying to replace the lamp. He chose to pay.

Sam wrote an amazing account of the incidents

you have just read about and handed it in as his history paper. For his work on *Blackbeard—Awful Pirate, More Awful Singer,* **Sam** earned an "F," the reputation of being a real wise guy, and a chance to write a makeup paper.

He still owes the makeup paper.

Jon Scieszka and **Lane Smith** collaborated on the best-selling ALA Notable Book *The True Story of the Three Little Pigs*. The author teaches at The Day School in Manhattan where he is known as Mr. Scieszka (mí · stər · shé · ska). He lives with his wife and two children in Brooklyn, where he is known as Dad (dæd).

Lane Smith's illustrations have appeared in magazines, newspapers, and on record album covers. He received a Silver Medal from the Society of Illustrators for *The True Story of the Three Little Pigs*. He lives in New York City, where most people can pronounce his name.